The Oleander Press Ltd
16 Orchard Street
Cambridge CB1 1JT
England

www.oleanderpress.co.uk

ISBN 978-0-90667-282-2

For Max on his first Christmas

One
Night
on
Earth

The angels sang in heaven,
A new day had begun.
God summoned the angel Gabriel
And said, "The time has come.
You must go on a journey,
You have some news to bear,
To a little town called Nazareth
And a young girl who lives there."

The young girl's name was Mary,
She was sweet and she was kind,
In fact the sweetest, kindest girl
That God could hope to find.
When Mary saw the angel
She stopped and stared with fear,
But smiling gently Gabriel said,
"There is a reason I am here:

Peace be with you Mary,
Don't look on me with fright.
The Lord your God has blessed you,
This is a joyous night.
You are to have a baby,
And the glorious news I bring
Is - he wont be just any child,
But God's own son - a King!

"You are to call him Jesus,
A name that means, 'God saves.'
This is so much for one so young
You must be strong and brave."
Mary said, "I can't have a baby,
I don't see how I can;
I am yet to marry Joseph,
A good and honest man."

"Have faith," said the angel Gabriel,
"God's spirit rests in you."
"I am his servant," Mary said,
"And will do what he wants me to."
That night Joseph had a dream
About Jesus being God's son;
How he should care for the child - protect him,
So that God's will could be done.

So Joseph married Mary
And when the baby was due,
They were told they should go to Bethlehem -
They had a lot of travelling to do.
Mary got tired and weary,
The road stretched on and on.
"We're nearly there now," Joseph said,
"My dear, we won't be long."

As Bethlehem came into sight
She moaned in pain and cried,
"Joseph! The baby is coming
And I'm so very tired!"
So Joseph banged on the door of an inn;
"No room!" The innkeeper said.
"The baby is coming," cried Mary again
"Somebody must have a bed?"

The very next inn was full as well,
So Joseph tried one more.
"Sorry we're full," that innkeeper said
And went to close the door.
But then he saw poor Mary;
"I do have a stable," he said,
"It's not great but it's available,
And the next best thing to a bed?"

The stable was full of cattle,
The innkeeper showed them inside.
"I'll take it," said Joseph quickly,
This wasn't a time for pride!
He herded the cows out of the way
And made Mary a bed on the floor.
There she gave birth to the son of God;
He squealed and cried in the straw.

Wrapping him up to keep him warm,
Mary kissed his little head,
Then laid him down in a manger
Where the animals were fed.
Joseph took care of Mary
And smiled down at the little one;
He welcomed Jesus to the world
And gave praise to God for his son.

More joyful than she had ever been,
Mary held Jesus tight;
She gazed with love as she fed him,
And settled him down for the night.
But the night was not yet over...
The door was opened again.
Mary could hear excited voices,
Then in walked several men.

She saw that the men were shepherds
As they came in holding their crooks;
They hurried to the manger
And all crowded round to look.
"Please excuse us," one said to Mary
"But this has been such a night!
We were minding our business and our sheep,
Then were blinded by this light.

"The light surrounded an angel,
God's son had been born, he said,
And he told us where we might find him,
And that he lay in a 'manger' bed.
We saw a host of angels,
Who filled the sky to sing:
'Praise to God and peace on Earth!'
So we rushed to find the new king."

They knelt and worshipped Jesus
And knew they had been blessed,
Then they left to go and spread the news
Leaving mother and baby to rest.
Joseph shut the stable door,
They were tired and ready for bed.
He said goodnight to Mary
And kissed Jesus on the head.

Far away in Jerusalem;
A king called Herod heard the news ~
Some wise men had come to his kingdom
In search of 'The King of the Jews'.
"I'm the King," thought Herod,
"And the only one there'll be.
If they find that child I should have him killed!
I'll have them bring him to me."

So he told them to find the baby
But pretended he was glad ~
Saying he wanted to worship him too,
Inside, jealousy driving him mad.
The wise men hurried on their way
And saw the brightest star,
"It's the sign," they said "let's follow it,
The baby can't be far."

The star blazed down from the heavens
Shining light on the stable door;
Rushing inside they found Jesus
And got down on their knees in the straw.
"We have travelled far," they said,
"We had some gifts to bring.
Gold and frankincense and myrrh,
To welcome the little king."

Soon after they said, "We must go home."
And kissed the baby's head.
They didn't return through Herod's land,
But went another way instead.
For on their way to Jesus,
God had told them in a dream
That Herod would hurt the baby,
And wasn't as good as he seemed!

Alone in the silence and the dark,
Mary gazed at her little boy;
She knew he was a miracle
And he filled her with love and joy.
She wondered how his life would be
As they both lay down to rest;
And as the mother of the son of God
She promised to do her best.

WHY NOT DRAW YOUR FAVOURITE
CHARACTERS FROM THE STORY
ON THESE PAGES?

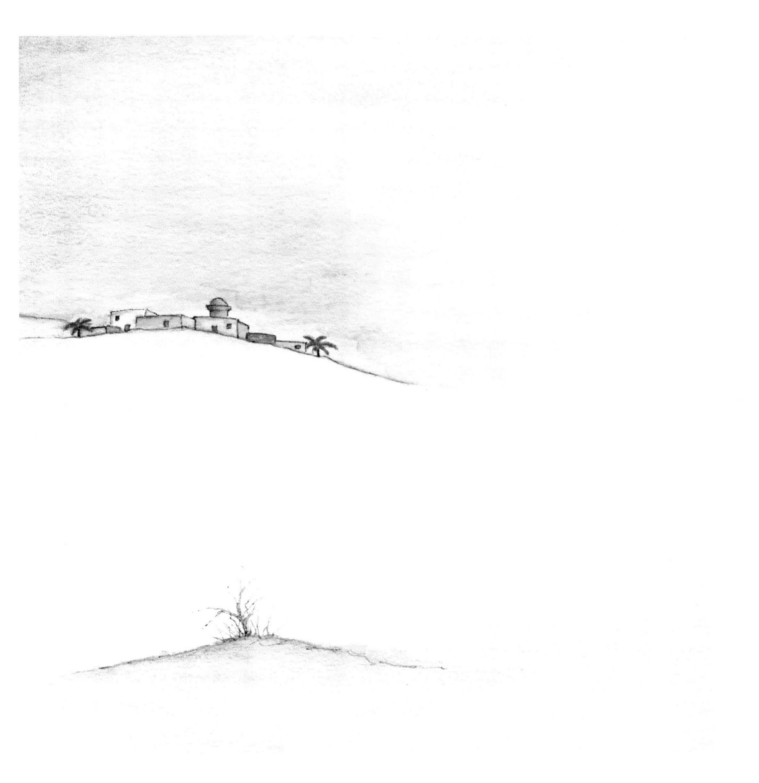

BE SURE TO CHECK OUT THE OTHER FABULOUS
CHILDREN'S STORIES AVAILABLE AT

WWW.OLEANDERPRESS.COM

Born in Northamptonshire in 1974, Leanne
Kilpatrick has colourful memories of
celebrating religious holidays with her vast
extended family. With Christianity playing
a large part in her own childhood, she
firmly believes that children today can
benefit from a basic understanding of its
teachings. In re-writing a collection of
much loved bible stories to rhyme, Leanne
hopes to convey their moral message and to
bring them vividly to life in the imagination
of the young reader or listener.

She lives in rural Warwickshire where she
lives with her husband Eric, sons James
and Sebastian, and a menagerie of dogs,
chickens, ducks and guinea fowl.

'One Night on Earth' is Leanne's second
children's book. Her royalties will be
donated to charity.

47169534R00016

Printed in Poland
by Amazon Fulfillment
Poland Sp. z o.o., Wrocław